D1165222

Sometimes you Fly

by Newbery Medalist
Katherine Applegate

Illustrated by
Jennifer Black Reinhardt

CLARION BOOKS
Houghton Mifflin Harcourt
Boston New York

For Lexie —K.A.

To my mom, who taught me to fly —J.B.R.

Clarion Books
3 Park Avenue
New York, New York 10016

Clarion Books is an imprint of Houghton Mifflin Harcourt Publishing Company.

hmhco.com

The illustrations in this book were done in ink and watercolor.
The text was set in Grandma.

Library of Congress Cataloging-in-Publication Data

Names: Applegate, Katherine, author. | Reinhardt, Jennifer Black, 1963- illustrator.
Title: Sometimes you fly / by Newbery Medalist Katherine Applegate ;
; illustrated by Jennifer Black Reinhardt.
Description: Boston ; New York : Clarion Books/Houghton Mifflin Harcourt,
[2018] | Summary: Illustrations and simple, rhyming text remind the reader
that any achievement may be preceded by mistakes, and learning from them
makes accomplishments sweeter.
Identifiers: LCCN 2017001026 | ISBN 9780547633909 (hardcover)
Subjects: | CYAC: Stories in rhyme. | Resilience (Personality
trait)—Fiction. | Persistence—Fiction.
Classification: LCC PZ8.3.A558 So 2018 | DDC [E]—dc23
LC record available at https://lccn.loc.gov/2017001026

Manufactured in China
SCP 10 9 8 7 6 5 4 3 2 1
4500691124

Before the cake . . .

before the peas . . .

before the laugh . . .

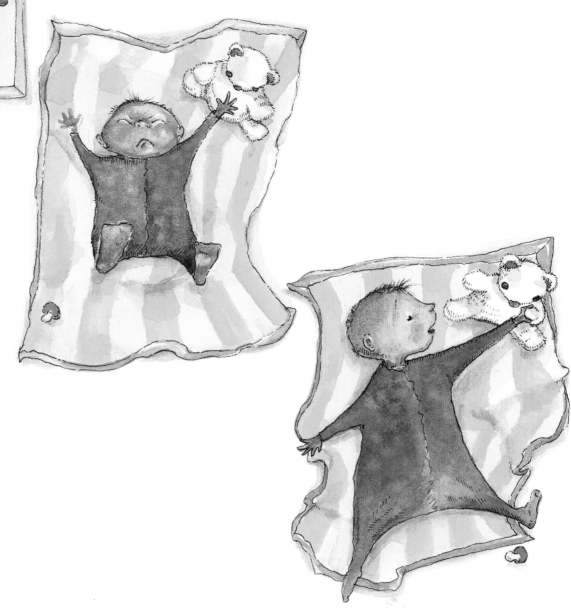

before the seas . . .

before the blocks . . .

before the grow . . .

before the friend . . .

before the know . . .

before the team . . .

before the ride . . .

before the heart . . .

before the pride . . .

Each recipe we undertake

can rise or fall,

can burn or bake.

But when we break
we learn to mend.

When breezes blow
we learn to bend.

Remember, then,
with every try,
sometimes you fail,

sometimes you fly.

What matters most

is what you take

from all you learn

before the cake.